CORA FLASH
and the Treasure of Beggar's Bluff

Tommy Davey

BROWN PAW
PRESS

ISBN: 1481216236
ISBN-13: 978-1481216234

CORA FLASH AND THE TREASURE OF BEGGAR'S BLUFF

ONE

I usually counted on the first day back at school being fairly exciting, but how could it compare to the thrills I'd experienced over the summer? I couldn't wait to see my friends so I could tell them all about the two mysteries I'd encountered in my summer off. I doubted very much that anyone else in my class would have a "What I did on my summer vacation" story that would top mine.

As I arrived in the yard of the school, I stopped to scan the kids standing around in groups talking about their summers. I recognized most of the kids, but there were definitely a few new faces, but mostly in the lower grades.

"Hi Cora," said a familiar voice.

I turned around to see Shelby Lane, who'd been my best friend since I was four.

"I'm so excited for this year, aren't you? I can't wait to get back into the swing of things, this year is going to be amazing!"

Shelby Lane stood slightly shorter than me but made up for the difference with her energetic personality and her frantic curly blonde hair. She talked so fast my mom would sometimes describe her as "headache-inducing."

"Hi Shelby. I don't know if I am as excited as you, but I guess I am a little excited."

I could not help but think the school year would pale drastically in comparison to my summer.

"Well, I am tremendously excited. Your email said you were going to tell me what happened to you this summer, but you wanted to wait until we saw each other in person. We're in person now, so tell me."

As close as Shelby and I were, I'd decided not to say anything to anyone about my mystery-filled adventures until I got back to school.

"Um... I got a dog."

Shelby's chin dropped and she looked at me

from underneath a raised eyebrow. "A dog? That's it? You said you had something exciting to tell me, you sounded like it was going to be the best story I have ever heard."

"It *is* exciting," I countered.

"I'm sure *you're* thrilled, but getting a dog is not as thrilling to others as you might think."

"I guess not," I said, allowing her to win the argument.

"I heard we have a new teacher," said Shelby. "His name is Mr. Levine and he is new in town, no one knows much about him. I heard that he was in prison."

"What?" I exclaimed. "Prison? There is no way he would have been in prison. They don't let ex-convicts teach school. That's the stupidest thing I have ever heard. Who told you that?"

"My mother," replied Shelby. "She heard from the school Superintendent, and you know that they are like that." She attempted to twist her index and middle fingers together in a sign of closeness. Unfortunately, she wasn't quite flexible enough, and she had to use her left hand to help her little fingers along.

"I think your mother is mistaken. She must have misunderstood," I said.

"Believe whatever you want, Cora Flash," said Shelby, "but I believe our teacher was in prison."

"Well, you're partially right," a voice boomed from behind us.

We turned around to see a man we did not recognize, looming down under a thick carpet of fuzzy black hair. We knew instantly it was our new teacher, the potential ex-convict.

"It's true, I was in prison – for a while," said Mr. Levine.

"You were?" asked a trembling Shelby.

"Yes," he laughed, "but it's not what you think. I was a teacher in the federal prison outside of town. I taught prisoners math and science for almost ten years."

"That sounds exciting," I said. "It must have been very interesting."

"Oh," he replied. "It was, but I decided it was time for a change, so I came back to teaching school."

I turned to Shelby and said, "I guess your mother misunderstood."

Shelby looked a little disappointed and more than a little embarrassed. "I guess so."

Knowing Shelby, she would probably give her mother a piece of her mind for letting her make such a fool of herself. She was very close to her mother, but they seemed to do an awful lot of their talking by yelling at each other.

"I'm Cora," I said to Mr. Levine, "Cora Flash. And this is Shelby Lane. I think we're both in your class this year."

"It's nice to meet you both, I'm sure we'll get to know each other very well over the school year. If you'll excuse me, I'm going to talk to a few more of the kids."

He walked away and joined a small circle of boys who were taking turns showing off their new sneakers.

"He seems nice," I said.

"Yeah," Shelby replied. "I guess so."

I could tell from the tone in her voice she was disappointed that our new teacher did not have a prison record, although I suspected her mother would be very relieved.

Just as I was about to ask Shelby about her summer, the outside bell rang.

"Let's line up," she said. "I want to be first."

She ran to the set of double doors that were saved for the upper grades and stood first in line. I stood behind her and watched the other kids from grade five fall in line behind us. Many of them said hello as they passed by; a few even stopped for hugs.

"Excuse me!" yelled Shelby. "Get to the back of the line!"

Jimmy Carson, our class clown, had the nerve to stand right in front of Shelby, taking her spot as first in line.

"I was here first," he said.

"You were not, Jimmy Carson!" yelled Shelby. "Now get to the back of the line!"

He turned around and smiled his sweet-as-syrup smile as he brushed the bangs out of his eyes.

"Shelby," he said, with his typical smirk, "don't you want me to be beside you? I thought we had something special."

I started laughing, not because Jimmy was particularly funny, but because I knew how upset his words would make Shelby.

"You're so immature!" she exclaimed. "Get out of here!"

She pushed him out of the line, causing him to lose his balance and fall right into Mr. Levine.

"Is there a problem here?" The teacher asked as he helped Jimmy upright.

"Yes," answered Shelby. "And his name is Jimmy Carson."

"I think everything is fine now," I said. "All sorted out."

"Good," said Mr. Levine, "then let's get going."

He looked at Jimmy and with a firm hand began to push him down the line. "To the end with you, young man."

Shelby smirked. She got to be first in line, keeping her perfect record for every first day of school.

TWO

"I am Mr. Levine," announced our new teacher from the front of the classroom. "I would appreciate your patience as I learn each of your names. Let's start by filling out one of these cards and standing it at the front of your desk."

Mr. Levine proceeded to walk around the classroom, passing out small tent cards for each of us to write our names.

"I hope he's nice," said Shelby from one seat behind me. "Not like that Mr. Giordano last year. He was mean."

"He wasn't mean," I countered. "He just didn't like people talking in his class, and you talk all the time."

Shelby sat back in her seat and wrote her name in a bright pink marker she had pulled out of her pencil case.

"This year," he began, "we are going to introduce you to the concept of the research project. You haven't done one in your last grade, so this will be a new thing for all of you."

Although I did not exactly understand what a research project entailed, it sounded right up my alley.

"What do we have to do?" asked Alex Bass from the back of the room.

"Please put up your hand first," said Mr. Levine.

Alex slowly raised his hand and waited.

"Yes?"

"What do we have to do?"

"For this project," explained the teacher, "you will each have a topic that you will need to research. Some of you will research on the Internet, some of you at the library. And others may decide to interview people for their assignment."

"This sounds like a lot of work," grumbled Shelby.

"I have written down topics on little pieces of paper and put them into this box. You will each draw one and have two weeks to research and present your findings to the class."

"Wait a minute," whispered Shelby. "We're getting homework? On the first day?"

Mr. Levine began to walk around the room, letting each of the students pull their assignment out of a shoebox.

When he got to me, I made sure to shuffle the pieces around. I let my fingers roll over the pieces of paper, feeling them pass under and between my fingers. Finally, I stopped on a piece that somehow felt better than the rest. I grabbed it and opened it.

"What did you get?" asked Shelby.

"Pick yours before I say," I replied.

She reached into the box and pulled out the first paper her fingers touched. She could not wait for me to open my paper, so she opened hers and read out the assignment: "Native edible plant species. What does that mean?"

"You have to research plants that are found in this area that we can eat," I said.

"Who eats plants?"

"We all do, like fruit and vegetables. They're considered part of the plant family."

"Vegetables?" she cried. "I have to do a project on vegetables? Oh brother."

Clearly Shelby was not impressed with her assignment. "What did you get? Dirt?"

I opened my piece of paper and read the contents. "The local shipping trade." I was not exactly sure what to make of it, but just as I was about to put my hand up to ask Mr. Levine, he appeared out of nowhere.

"This area used to be a very active shipping port, the river was very busy up until the railroad was built. Many ships passed through this area, and it's your job to find out where they were going, or where they came from."

"Oh," I said. That sounded more interesting than vegetables.

"Wow," said Shelby, after Mr. Levine had moved on. "This guy sure knows how to bore a bunch of kids."

Despite what Shelby thought, I couldn't wait to get started on my assignment.

□

THREE

"Cora," said my Mom, "this new job I have means I am going to need you to help out at home a bit more."

We were sitting at the dinner table talking about my mother's new job. She had just started working as an insurance claims inspector after working in insurance sales for many years. It was higher pay, but would mean more time away from me and my two-year-old brother Ethan.

"I already help out," I said. "I do lots."

"I know you do, sweetie," she said to me, "but

there are going to be some evenings and weekends where I need you to watch over Ethan if I have to investigate an accident or claim scene. And until your father gets back from the road, you are my number two."

My father traveled a lot, mostly to other states, selling broadband Internet service to businesses. He always said the life of the salesman was nothing but airport lounges and lousy hotels. My mother's new job, however, sounded terribly exciting, even a little bit dangerous. She was the person who would be responsible for looking into people's insurance claims to make sure they were telling the truth. If she determined the claims were valid, she would approve their request and pay the insurance amount. For some of the claims, there were hundreds of thousands of dollars at stake. She was almost like a detective, which thrilled me to bits.

"I understand," I said. "I can take care of Ethan, don't worry."

Almost as if he'd been waiting for the chance, Ethan took a handful of his dinner and threw it across the room. Mashed potatoes and green peas were suddenly all over the kitchen floor.

"Ethan!" my mom yelled. "Stop that!"

Ethan found humor in his actions and began to

laugh hysterically.

"I'll get it," I said, reaching for the paper towels to begin the cleanup operation.

"Thank you, Cora," she said.

I started to wipe up the mess, but it felt more like I was just pushing it around the floor into a big blobby pile. "Eww, gross," I said out loud.

Calvin, my Norfolk Terrier, sprang into action at the opportunity for more food, gobbling up as many of the mashed potatoes and peas as he could manage.

"Calvin, stop it," I said, trying to push him out of the way. He forcefully fought back, pushing his snout into the mashed potatoes, licking furiously the whole time.

After I had the mess cleaned up, I sat back down and started to tell my mother about the assignment we'd received from Mr. Levine.

"Homework on your first day?"

"You sound like Shelby," I laughed. "It's just a research project. I have to learn about the shipping trade from this area. I'll need to go to the library after dinner, I'm going to meet Shelby there."

"Okay," Mom replied. "I'll take you after dinner. Can you ask Shelby's dad to drive you home? I'll be putting Ethan to bed."

I didn't think Shelby's dad would mind driving me home; he often drove me home when Shelby and I went to the movies.

"Do you have your first case yet?" I asked my mom.

"I do, but I'm not supposed to talk about it."

"Oh come on!" I cried. "Who am I going to tell?"

"I know," she said with a giggle. "I'll tell you, but you can't repeat this to anyone you know. You never know if one of the people involved is related to someone at school."

"I promise!"

"Well," she began, "the number seventeen bus was driving up Water Street a few weeks ago and a car cut off the bus quite suddenly. The driver of the bus stopped and avoided hitting the car, but many of the passengers were hurt."

"That's terrible," I said.

"It is. And there are many claims from the passengers, eight in all, who have medical expenses that they would like to have covered."

"It sounds scary," I said. "Was anyone seriously hurt?"

"Thankfully, no. The injuries are mostly whiplash and a few broken bones, but nothing very serious."

I was intrigued by my Mom's first case on the job. "So what do you have to do?"

"Well, I'm going to start by interviewing each of the passengers on the bus, as well as the driver of the bus."

"What about the driver of the car who cut them off?"

"Unfortunately, that person left the scene, so I won't be able to get any information from them. But remember, I'm not the police. I'm not trying to find out who caused the accident. I just need to find out if the passengers have a legitimate claim to medical compensation."

"Compensation?" I asked.

"Payment," Mom explained. "Money, basically. I have to determine if the insurance company will cover their medical expenses. Okay, let's get going."

My mom scooped Ethan up from his highchair and grabbed her purse from the kitchen island. "I'll clean up after I get home," she said. "Do you have your library card?"

I arched my eyebrow, clearly indicating that her question was preposterous. "I always have my library card with me," I said as we walked out the front door.

FOUR

The town library, one of the oldest on the east coast, was one of the many libraries built with money from millionaire Andrew Carnegie in the early 1930s. I had spent many days in the library, spread out on the floor reading mystery after mystery. Sometimes the librarian, Mr. Burton, would have to tell me to leave as I had stayed well past closing time.

Shelby had agreed to meet me at the library, but she'd sent me a text to say she was running behind because her mom was caught up watching *Jeopardy*, yelling answers at the screen and refusing to leave until the program ended.

I decided to take advantage of the extra time and see if there were any new mysteries to check out. The library collection was not vast, but they managed to add enough new titles each month to keep me happy. A shelf near the front always had all the new books on display. As usual, three or four sounded appealing to me.

I picked up, *The Mystery of the Golden Leopard.* It sounded a bit ridiculous. Who ever heard of a golden leopard?

"It's a statue," said a voice behind me.

I turned around to see the librarian, Mr. Burton, standing nearby.

"The book," he continued. "It's about a golden statue shaped like a leopard that goes missing."

"Oh," I said. "That sounds intriguing."

"I don't think you'll like it," he added. "It's not very well-plotted. You know right from the beginning who the culprit is."

Mr. Burton was right. I would not like that book at all. One of my biggest pet peeves was to know the end of the book almost from the beginning. I replaced the book and continued browsing.

"This one you will like," he said, handing me

another.

I took it from him and read the title out loud, "*The Crystal Caper*. Wow, that does sound exciting. Have you read it?"

"No, not yet, but some other patrons have told me it was one of the best stories they have read in a long time. I think you should give it a try."

That was enough reason for me, so I tucked the book under my arm and made a mental note to check it out.

"Can we get this over with?" said Shelby, who'd suddenly appeared by my side.

"Hi. I'm ready if you are."

"Cora, do you want to trade topics? I think you'd do much better with this one than I would."

"No way. I'm quite happy with my subject. Let's go look for some books and we'll meet back at one of the big tables."

"Fine," she said. "I'm going to need some help," she said to Mr. Burton.

"What exactly are you looking for?" he asked.

"Here," she said, handing him the slip of paper with her topic on it. "I have to do a report on this."

He took the paper from her hands and studied it closely. "Ah, well, that is quite interesting. Come with me and I'll show you where to look."

She followed Mr. Burton and disappeared into the stacks in search of books on local vegetation.

I had been to the library so many times that I knew exactly where to start looking for my books. I skipped over to the section on local history and started to scan the shelves for anything that might help.

There were not many books to choose from, and in fact only one seemed worth reading. *"Shipping Routes of the East Coast."* Maybe it wouldn't have anything for my area, since it covered the whole East Coast, but I thought I'd look through it to see if anything caught my eye. It was a pretty large book, so I hauled it back to one of the project tables.

SLAM! The book fell onto the desk with a loud thump, startling everyone in the otherwise silent room.

"Sorry," I whispered loudly. "It was an accident."

I sat down at the table and began to flip through the massive book. It was very thorough, covering many different regions, each represented by a number of maps.

"Finally," I said as I discovered the part of the book that covered our town.

I began to skim through the description of

industries that used the river to ship their goods to and from our region. There were a number of references to salt and flour refineries, making it sound like our town was the best place for a baker to live.

I turned the page and noticed a small piece of paper tucked into the middle part, the gutter, of the book.

"Ugh," said Shelby as she joined me, dropping a pile of books on the table. "Can you believe all of these books? There are ten or twelve of them, and I have to read them all."

"Shhhh!" said a man two tables away.

"Sorry," she said in a tone that didn't sound very apologetic. "What is that?" she asked, noticing the small piece of paper in my hands.

"I found it tucked into this book."

I started to open the paper, unfolding it until I could read the message written inside, *"Fortune and love favor the brave. CMXLVI JON."*

"What does that mean?"

"I'm not sure."

I stared at the last part for a long time. CMXLVI JON. What could that mean? Some sort of code, I guessed. But for what?

FIVE

That night, I sat in front of the computer and typed in the code written on the piece of papery I'd found. CMXLVI JON.

I hit search and browsed the results that appeared on screen. There were quite a few references to CMXLVI, but nothing that paired it with JON. I could not find a link between the two things.

Next, I tried searching on the rest of the message, "Fortune and love favor the brave." That one uncovered many hits, and it became clear that the quote was from a Roman poet named Ovid who died in AD 17.

I tried saying it out loud to see if it made any sense. "Fortune and love favor the brave."

"Reading poetry?" Mom asked from the doorway.

"Yeah," I said, not wanting to get into the details of my discovery.

"How did your library search go?"

"Okay, but I only found one helpful book. I think I might need to look up some stuff on the Internet."

My mother shook her head, "I doubt you'll find that much online. I remember when we first decided to move here, we tried to search for information on the local area and did not find much at all."

That disappointed me a great deal. If I couldn't find anything on the Internet, I wasn't sure where to go next.

"You know who you could talk to? Mr. French, at the Town Hall. He curates the little museum that is in the lobby."

That little museum was nothing more than a bookcase, mounted to the wall with three or four black-and-white pictures of the area, and a few bricks from the original town hall that had burned down in the 1920s.

"Maybe. I could try," I replied.

Mom disappeared as quickly as she'd appeared, and I continued my search to make sense of the CMXLVI.

Wait a second, I thought to myself. *I know what these are!*

Something clicked in my head and I suddenly remembered seeing letters arranged like this before. They were numbers, but not normal numbers that we use today. Roman numerals!

I quickly searched, "CMXLVI Roman numerals" and up popped a whole bunch of answers. They all pointed to the same thing. CMXLVI stands for 946. I read the message again, "Fortune and love favor the brave. 946 JON."

I wasn't entirely sure that figuring out the Roman numerals had made a difference. 946 JON was too short to be code for a phone number, so what else could it stand for?

Blip! My computer announced an incoming message from Shelby.

"Hi," I typed.

"I'm so bored," she responded. "I hate this project."

"Give it a chance," I typed. "You just started!"

"I think Mr. Levine hates us. Why else would he give us homework on the first day?"

"That's normal for our grade," I responded. "We'll probably get homework every single day, and weekend."

"I have to go back to the library tomorrow," she answered. "There's one more book I have to check out. Do you want to come?"

The library. Of course, that was it!

"I have to log off," I hastily typed.

I closed the chat window and looked at the sticky note in front of me.

946 JON.

It was a code, and I knew exactly what for. I had to go back to the library the next day to find a new book.

SIX

I was not able to concentrate much at school the day after figuring out my coded message.

Twice Mr. Levine stopped speaking to ask me if I was okay. Both times, I'd turned my head toward the wall and let my eyes glaze over. He must have thought I was bored, or focused on something unrelated to his lesson plans. Both times, I apologized and tried to refocus.

"Are you coming to the library after school?" Shelby asked as we prepared to go for lunch.

"Of course!" I responded, with no attempt to

hide my enthusiasm. "I can't wait to get there."

"It's just the library, not the Dairy Palace."

The Dairy Palace was our favorite ice cream shop. We often met there on Saturdays to talk about our friends and trade gossip.

"I'm going to the lunch room now," Shelby announced, taking her knapsack from under her desk. "You coming?"

"Yeah." I grabbed my bag and followed her out the door.

"Just a minute," said Mr. Levine. "Cora, can I talk to you before you go to lunch?"

"Uh oh," said Shelby, under her breath. "It's the second day and you're already in trouble."

Shelby left the room and I walked up to Mr. Levine's desk. "Yes?"

"Cora, I know we have just met," he began. "But you seem a little lost today. Is something wrong?"

"I'm just thinking about my school project."

"Really?" he sounded genuinely surprised.

"Yeah, honest. Well, sort of. When I was researching my project, I discovered something else that interested me. It's a bit of a puzzle that I am trying to figure out."

"That sounds intriguing. Maybe you will present your second project to the class if it turns out to be as puzzling as it sounds."

"Maybe, but I've just started looking into it. It might turn out to be nothing."

Those words pained me. I felt awful that the clue on the small piece of paper might not turn out to be anything meaningful. At the same time, I only had a hunch that might not have led anywhere.

"Go for lunch then, and enjoy."

Every day for as long as I had been at the same school, I'd sat with Shelby and our friend Tricia Morgan. Tricia was in the same grade as us, but in a different class. There were an unusual number of eleven-year-olds in our school, so we were split into two separate classes, but we all knew each other and hung out.

"I heard your teacher was in jail," said Tricia.

"No, he wasn't," said Shelby. "He taught at a prison. He was not a prisoner."

I couldn't help but think it ironic that Shelby was deflecting the accusation against Mr. Levine since she'd started the rumor in the first place!

"Oh," said Tricia, sounding a little disappointed. "I guess that's different."

"What are you doing this weekend?" I asked.

"We are going sailing. Do you want to come?"

"Yeah!" I yelled.

"My mom told me to ask you," she said.

"Well I want to come, too!" cried Shelby. "Can I come?"

"Yes," Tricia said. "You are also invited."

Shelby's depressed expression immediately turned into a smile. "Thank you," she said graciously.

"That might help my project," I said. "I have to research shipping routes in our region. We'll be sailing right through the same areas. I can take some pictures to use for my presentation."

"You're showing pictures in your presentation?" asked Shelby. "Ugh, I can't show pictures of vegetables in my presentation. I'll get laughed at!"

"What time should we be ready?" I asked.

"We'll pick you up at nine on Saturday. Have a good breakfast before we get there."

We finished our lunch talking about the new boy in Tricia's class. Nathan, or something like that.

The rest of the day went by just as painfully slow as the first part. I could not wait for it to end so I could get over to the library and start searching for the answer to my clue!

SEVEN

As soon as the bell rang at the end of the school day, I grabbed my bag and ran to the door calling after Shelby. "Let's go!"

"Well wait for me, at least!" she yelled.

I really wanted to run all the way to the library, but Shelby was not interested in high-tailing it with me.

"Why are you so excited to research your project, anyway?" she asked. "Is shipping that interesting?"

"I don't know," I said, "I'm just anxious to get

started. I don't like to leave anything to the last minute."

That was the truth, and she knew it. I was always prepared and had my work done well ahead of schedule, most of the time. Shelby, on the other hand, often did not get started on things until the night before they were due! Surprisingly, she was able to get good grades and managed to stay out of trouble.

The library was a bit quieter than the night before; we were earlier and most people were still at work. It would be easy to search for the book I needed without people getting in the way.

"I'll see you at the tables later," I said to Shelby as I made my way to the back of the library.

"Okay," she said. "Try not to be too excited. It is a library after all."

I took out the piece of paper I'd found the night before and looked at the clue once more. *"Fortune and love favor the brave. CMXLVI JON."* The last part, which I'd determined to mean 946 JON is the reason I had to return to the library.

I knew that books in the library were filed under the Dewey Decimal system. Children's books were assigned a three-digit number followed by the first three letters of the author's last name. I guessed that

946 JON was the call number for a book. The clue I found in the shipping book was leading me to another book, in section 946.

Slowly, I walked down the bookcases until I came to the 900 section. I knew the 900 section had the history books, but I was not sure what the 940's section was. I started to see books that started with 940, and they appeared to be about the history of Europe.

As I made my way down the shelves, I saw books on Britain, then Germany, France and Italy. Next in the list was Spain, and all the books on Spain started with – 946!

Next, I began to skim the books to find ones that had JON as the first letters of the author's last name. There were only two, *The History of Ancient Spain* by Amanda Jonas, and *Spain's Enemies* by Steven Jones. I took both books off the shelf and started to flip through them, looking for anything that might be noteworthy.

The first book, *The History of Ancient Spain* contained no writing or notes tucked into the spine. I placed it down on the floor beside me and began to flip through the second book.

Near the back of the book, something did not seem right. Two of the pages appeared to be glued together. They were a bit thicker and stiff. I looked at the pages closely, and could see a spot where the glue was not right to the edge. Using my fingernail, I pried the two pages apart, and discovered the glue only ran around the edges of each of the pages, almost like a frame.

This left a spot in the middle of the pages where there was no glue—a perfect place for someone to tuck a small folded piece of paper.

I reached into the gap and pulled out the note someone had left. After unfolding it, I could not believe my eyes.

It appeared to be a treasure map, or half of one–hand drawn, with part of the map seeming to be water, a river or lake. There were no labels, so I couldn't tell what area the map illustrated. A single red 'X' was drawn over some jagged lines next to the water, cliffs or mountains of some sort.

Suddenly, I heard a noise from the other side of the bookshelf. I peeked through to find another pair of eyes looking back at me!

I let out a slight scream and dropped the book where I'd found the note. I made sure to hold on tightly to the map as I ran around to the other side of the shelf, but by the time I got around to the other side, the person had disappeared. I ran to the end of the row just in time to see a man in a beige trench coat run out the front door of the library.

"Wait!" I called out.

Mr. Burton wasn't behind the counter, so I couldn't ask him if he knew the man in the beige coat.

I could only stand helplessly in the middle of the library wondering who had been spying on me, and if he was after what I'd found.

A treasure map.

EIGHT

"Calvin, we have a treasure map!" I exclaimed. My dog responded by energetically wagging his tail.

Curiously, one half of the map appeared to be torn, but there was a big red X on the half that I had. A blue line pointed from the red 'X' to some words, "REE WISE" and "OW ALL" underneath. The first few letters of the writing must have been on the other side of the map, the half I didn't have.

"Whatcha got there?" asked my mom as she entered my room.

"It's nothing. Just a map."

"For your school project?"

"Yeah."

I wasn't in the habit of lying to my mother, but I had a feeling she wouldn't be too thrilled with me going on a treasure hunt, especially after my recent adventures with the Diamond of Madagascar and a close call with a ghost in Mount Topaz. I decided to not worry her by telling her about my latest finding. It might, after all, turn out to be nothing.

What could the treasure be? Gold? Jewels? Maybe pirate treasure—a chest with priceless coins, rubies and gold chains overflowing onto the ground. I had seen too many pirate movies! Did my area even have pirates? Could that have been a possibility?

I grabbed the book on shipping routes I'd checked out of the library. Maybe pirates would be mentioned in there.

Flipping through the book, I found the reference to my region. The first paragraph of the section said:

The Filbert River was used mainly in the early 1800's and into the mid part of the century. After the railroads were built, shipping by river in this area declined heavily. The water levels changed frequently due to the runoff from main tributaries, and although this was controlled in the 1920s with the building of a dam, most of the transport had already shifted away to the railroads and the industry never recovered.

That sounded interesting, but said nothing about pirates. I skimmed through the rest of the section, mostly looking for the word "Pirate" or "Shipwreck", but did not see anything.

I started to research pirates on the Internet, and discovered they were actually a very serious threat in the heyday of shipping, with some believing it began when the first boats hit the water. Modern-day pirates were still active in some parts of the world, even now.

That night, I dreamed about pirates, and treasure and what I would do with all of the gold coins and jewels if I found them. Even though modern day pirates seemed to operate far away from where we lived, there was still the possibility that the map led to a stolen treasure... but what could the treasure be?

NINE

I returned home from school the next day to an empty house. Mom was still out with Ethan, so I'd have to take Calvin on his walk.

The year before, my mom had given me my own key so I could let myself in after school. It took a lot of convincing for her to let me stay on my own, but I hated when she made me go to Mrs. Trumble's house until she got back. Mrs. Trumble was nice, but all she ever had to drink was ginger ale and that always reminded me of when I had my tonsils out. I'd gotten sick of it the first day.

As soon as I entered the house, Calvin jumped up on me and started licking my face, his version of giving kisses. I thanked him with a gentle squeeze and reached for his leash, which we kept conveniently beside the front door.

I left my knapsack sitting by the front door, deciding to deal with it after we returned.

"Come on, Calvin," I said, leading him out the door.

Our typical walk only lasted about ten minutes. We would walk down about six or seven houses, not even making it as far as the corner, before Calvin would start pulling his leash, asking to be taken back home. I wasn't entirely sure if Calvin was a lazy dog, or just very stubborn.

On our way back, Calvin stopped a few times to relieve himself and endlessly sniff at leaves or grass until I pulled him away with a, "Let's go!" After a few minutes, I decided it was time to head home.

I unlocked the front door and let Calvin in ahead of me, unhinging him from his leash so he could tear about the house looking for one of his many toys. I picked up my knapsack from the hallway and headed for my room.

When I pushed open my bedroom door, I was shocked to see my room in a complete mess. My drawers were opened and turned out on the floor. My sheets were pulled right off the bed and thrown in a pile. The books I had carefully alphabetized on my bookcase had been dumped in a jumbled pile under my window.

My first thought was that Ethan had gotten inside my room and decided to pull things apart. My mom obviously had not noticed before she left, or she would have tidied it up.

"Ethan!" I shouted. "Ugh!"

As I started to pick up the books on the floor, I heard a noise from somewhere else in the house.

"Mom?" I called.

No answer.

I opened the door to my room and tiptoed out to the kitchen.

"Mom? Is that you?"

A crash thundered from the bathroom, the door flew open and someone came tearing out. The intruder pushed passed me, covering his face as he ran out the sliding doors at the back of the kitchen.

Calvin, clearly realizing this person should not have been in our house, began to hysterically bark at him.

The man ran out the doors with Calvin hot on his trail.

"Calvin!" I yelled as I took after them both.

I ran out the door just in time to see the man jump over the bushes that separated us from the row of houses on the next street.

Calvin was far too small to jump over the bushes himself, but he continued to bark furiously in the direction of the intruder.

The intruder, I could not help notice, had been wearing a beige trench coat, just like the man who was watching me at the library. It did not take me long to realize what the man was looking for. He was clearly after the treasure map.

TEN

"What do you mean there was a man in the house?" Mom yelled.

Twenty minutes had passed and she and Ethan had returned home. We were standing in the kitchen along with Officer Orzabal. As soon as I'd come back inside, I'd called the police, even before calling my mother to tell her to come home.

"Who was he?"

"I don't know. I came home, went to my room and noticed it looked like someone had gone through some things. When I went into the kitchen, the man pushed passed me and ran out the back door. Calvin tried to chase him, but he didn't catch him."

"You've got yourself a regular little police dog," Officer Orzabal said.

"Yeah," I replied. "He's pretty good at catching criminals, but not this time."

"Aarrgh," said Calvin, slumping to the floor, clearly disappointed that he hadn't caught the intruder.

"You're sure you're okay?" Mom said to me.

"I'm fine, really."

"What was he looking for?"

"That's what we're trying to figure out," said Officer Orzabal. "From what we can see, nothing was taken from the house. Your jewelry wasn't touched, and neither was your laptop. And since both were in plain view, he would not have had any trouble finding them. And for some reason he seemed to be concentrating on Cora's room."

My Mom threw up her hands. "Why would he want to search through the room of an eleven-year-old girl?"

"Maybe he likes *Nancy Drew* books," joked the Officer.

"Cora," my Mom said, ignoring the Officer's

attempt at making a joke. "Do you know what he might have been looking for?"

"No," I lied. "I can't think of anything." I couldn't help but think of the treasure map that was safely tucked away in my knapsack, but decided not to say anything in case the police decided to take the map. Luckily the intruder hadn't noticed it sitting beside the front door.

"Well," said Officer Orzabal, "here's my card if you think of anything. I'm going to drive around the neighborhood for a while in case I see anything suspicious. Call me at the first sign of anything strange."

My mother took the card from his outstretched hand. "Thank you," she said, "I will. And tomorrow, we're getting a security system installed."

"Have a good night, try not to let this bother you too much," said the Officer as he left our house.

"Isn't that a laugh?" said Mom. "How could we not let this bother us? Someone broke into our home!"

"I'm sure it was just random," I said. "They were looking for something and didn't find it, so they moved on. I'm sure it's done now."

"I hope you're right, Cora, because I don't feel safe right now."

Mom turned and went into the kitchen, locking the sliding doors with great force. She took a broom from the kitchen cupboard and wedged it into the doorframe for extra support.

"I'm going to start cooking dinner now," she said.

"Okay," I replied. "I'm just going to tidy up a bit."

I returned to my room and stared at the mess on the floor, still feeling guilty for lying. Not only had I lied to my Mom, I'd lied to a police officer! I'm pretty sure lying to the police is a punishable offense, but lying to Mom carries a much harsher punishment!

Calvin sniffed around the room and growled a little as he detected the scent of the intruder.

"I know, Calvin. Don't worry, we'll find out who he is."

Sitting on the edge of my stripped bed, I took out the map again. The red X was clearly marked over some hills or mountains, but the blue line that pointed from the red X and led to the scramble of letters over the torn half of the page clearly had something important to do with the treasure.

I *had* to find the other half of the map.

ELEVEN

That night when I returned home, a truck marked 'Bulletproof Security Agency' was parked in the driveway.

Inside, Mom was grilling the poor little man from Bulletproof on whether or not their product lived up to their name. "Do you sell electric fences?" she asked. "You know, the kind they have in prisons?"

"Mom," I interrupted. "I think that's a little extreme."

"Don't worry Mrs. Flash," said the Bulletproof

man, "the system that I have picked out for you is almost as good as having an electric fence. There will be motion sensors on every window and door. No one can come in or out of here without tripping the alarm system. You can also have cameras set up so you can see who is in your house at any time of the day right from your computer or phone."

"I don't want a camera in my room," I said.

"No, we don't put them in the rooms, unless you want them," he said. "We just put them on the main entrances and exits, as well as the exterior of the house."

"I guess that sounds good," said Mom. "Can you do it today?"

"Absolutely. Let me just get my stuff out of the truck."

The Bulletproof man left the house to get his materials so he could begin converting our house into Fort Knox.

Bling! My computer made a noise to alert me that Shelby was sending a video message. I clicked 'connect' and watched my screen fill with a full-size video of Shelby's face.

"Hi," she said.

"Hey."

"I heard what happened. How did you hear

about that?"

"Officer Orzabal ran into my dad at the coffee shop, he told him all about the break in."

"Why didn't you tell me?"

"I didn't want anyone to worry," I replied.

"What do you think they were looking for?"

I thought a minute before answering. Shelby Lane had the biggest mouth in school. I knew there was a fifty-fifty chance she would text message everyone within minutes of our conversation ending.

"You have to promise you won't say anything," I finally said.

Shelby's eyes lit up like the headlights of a new car. "Of course! I swear!"

"The other night, when we were at the library, I found a map—or part of one at least."

"What kind of map?" Her eyes widened even more than before, which I would have not thought possible.

"I'm not sure. But it has a big red X on it."

"It's a treasure map!" she squealed. "You found a treasure map!"

"I don't know for sure that it's a treasure map, or if it's even real. And besides, half the map is missing."

"Do you know who has the other half of the map?"

"No."

She gasped. "And you think the person who broke into your house is the person who has the other half of the map?"

"I'm beginning to think so. Why else would someone break into my house and not bother with anything valuable? They only searched my room, and since I had the map with me, there was nothing to be found."

"Cora, you need to tell the police about the map!"

I shook my head. "Not just yet. I have to see if I can find out who has the other half before I tell anyone."

"I don't think that is a very good idea," she said, "but if you go searching for it, I want to come with you."

"Of course. I'm going to go now. I have some things to do."

I told my Mom I was taking Calvin for a long walk, but I would be back in a while. I made sure to take my cell phone in case she panicked and wanted to know exactly where I was.

I ended up down by the waterfront, so I could

take some pictures of the river for my project. As I stood by the docks, with Calvin at my side, a voice spoke from beside me. "Well hello there."

I turned around to see a fisherman in his full gear. He looked just like the man on the box of frozen fish sticks that my mom bought for Ethan.

"Hi there," I said.

"Aarf!" said Calvin, introducing himself.

"You're the Flash girl, aren't you?" he said.

"Yes, I am." Apparently he knew my parents.

"I'm Gerald Pape. Your dad used to work for me in the summers to make some cash when he was in school."

I'd never pictured my father as a fisherman before, so I found this piece of trivia very amusing. "I never knew that. Was he any good?"

"Nah, not really, but he was an extra pair of hands, and that's what mattered. What are you doing down here by yourself?"

"Aargh," growled Calvin, offended at having been left out.

"Not by yourself, then," corrected Gerald. "What are you doing here with your dog?"

As if satisfied with Gerald's new question, Calvin settled down at my feet.

"I'm doing a project for school," I answered.

"About shipping routes."

"Ah, well they don't ship much here anymore. All the industry is gone."

"That's what I've learned."

"Even the fishing has mostly disappeared. I'm one of the only guys around here now, and some days I wonder if I should pack it in." Gerald seemed saddened by the thought of giving up his livelihood. He lowered his head and started kicking the side of his left boot with the other foot.

"I'm sure things will pick up," I said. I was not exactly sure what I meant by that, but my dad would often say that to local businessmen when they were telling him how slow business was.

"Were there ever any... pirates around here?" I asked.

Gerald laughed. "Pirates? Good heavens, no. Not around here."

"Oh," I said, disappointed.

"I know pirates are very exciting to folks your age, but they were a dangerous bunch in their day. Many people lost their lives to the sword of a pirate."

"I just thought there might have been some here because of all the shipping."

"No, I'm afraid not. All of the industry here was

established long after the time that any pirates would have been around. Although they would have had quite a bounty in this area, there was a lot of gold that was taken through this river."

"Gold?"

"That's right. There were a number of gold mines up river, four or five of them I believe. There's nothing left in them now, but there was quite a bit of it for a time. The gold would have been transported by ship along the river, right through here. Millions of dollars' worth."

"Did any of it go missing?" I asked.

"There was a story," he began, "about one of the ships disappearing. In the middle of the night, the ship vanished. Not sure if it sank, or if it changed course and got lost, but it was never heard of again."

"And the gold was never found?"

"Not as far as I know. I think they believed the crew purposely changed course and ended up somewhere else far away from here, keeping the gold to themselves."

"That's interesting," I said.

"Will that help your project?" Gerald asked.

"Yes, it certainly will!"

Even though I only had one half of the treasure

map, at least I knew what I was looking for.

A boatload of gold. That certainly sounded like a lost treasure to me.

TWELVE

That night at dinner, I decided to quiz Mom about her first case at her new job. "Any developments on your case?"

"Nothing interesting. I've interviewed five of the eight passengers, and they all have notes from their doctor and therapists, all with proper documentation. So far no evidence of fraud."

"You sound disappointed," I said.

"I am, a little. Isn't that terrible? I was hoping there would be a fraud claim that I discovered, and saved the company some money."

"That would make you look good."

"Yes, and I want to make a good impression," she said. "It's a new job and I want to do well."

I noticed a file folder on the dining table with the label, "NUMBER 17 BUS, WATER ST."

"Is that the bus accident file?" I asked.

"Yes, I have to review it again after dinner."

"Can I take a look through it?" I wasn't sure she'd let me, but decided to take a shot anyway.

"I don't know, it's privileged information. I could get in trouble."

I looked around the room. "The only other person in the room is Ethan," I said looking at my brother in his highchair. He was busy throwing carrots on the ground, which Calvin eagerly gobbled up. "I think you're safe here, Mom."

"Okay, I suppose."

Mom cleared the dinner table as I began to look through the notes she'd taken in her interviews.

"Your handwriting is really messy," I said. "Mr. Levine would make you do writing exercises if he saw this."

"Just read," she said, loading the dishwasher.

I started to scan the medical files of each of the people and couldn't help notice the same name come up a few times.

"Mom," I said. "Three of these people you have interviewed have the same doctor. Dr. Crawley signed the medical certificates for all but two of these people."

"Really?" she said, wiping her hands and coming over to the table. "Let me see that."

I gave her the papers and watched a puzzled look appear on her face.

"Well how do you like that? It sounds like you may have found something."

"It seems like an awful coincidence that three of the victims have the same doctor, doesn't it?"

Mom's expression turned to one of uncertainty. "Maybe not," she said. "This is not a very big town, so it could be possible. Especially if the bus they were travelling on passed by the area where the doctor's office is located."

"It sounds like you have some investigating to do," I said.

"It sure does."

She wasn't the only one who had some investigating ahead of her that evening. I had to find out more about that missing boat full of gold.

As soon as I was finished cleaning the counter and wiping off the table, I hurried to my room and started to research the gold.

I searched for anything that had to do with 'gold' or 'boat' 'river' 'missing' but couldn't find very much. I found many other stories of boats that went missing, or rivers that had gold in them, but not in a way that would help me.

Just as I was about to give up, I found an article about a woman who'd been married to one of the sailors on the boat. A journalist had interviewed her shortly after the gold disappeared. Someone had scanned it and uploaded a picture of it on a website all about missing money.

It was hard to make out all of the words, as the article was old and hadn't scanned very well. I strained to read some of the contents of the interview:

Evening Star: Mrs. Gordon, do you think there was a mutiny on board? Was the gold stolen by one or more of the crewmembers?

Maggie: Lyle would have told me if there were others on the boat who were looking to steal that gold. He wouldn't have just disappeared with it.

Evening Star: It has been almost a year since the S.S. Guppy disappeared. Have you heard anything from Lyle?

Maggie: I certainly have not. I know what people are saying, that he and the rest of the crew took the gold and ran off somewhere, but I don't believe it. I think the boat sank, and they were lost at sea. It pains me to think of all of those men, good men, dying that way, but I can't believe it happened any other way.

With the one-year passing of the disappearance of the S.S. Guppy, authorities have officially called off the search for the missing boat, its men and cargo. Maggie still holds out hope that one day her husband Lyle will return, with or without the gold.

I printed the article in case I needed to refer back to it, wondering what ever became of Maggie and Lyle Gordon.

THIRTEEN

"Will you come with me?" I asked Shelby the next day at school.

"Who is this person again?"

I repeated the story of the missing boat and Maggie and Lyle Gordon. I told her that with a little bit of Internet research, I'd managed to track down Maggie Gordon and wanted to visit her to see if she knew anything about the missing boat.

"I'm going to go by her house on my way home from school. She might know something about the treasure."

"Fine," Shelby said, "but if she gives you a reward for having the treasure map, I get half."

"I am not going to tell her I have the map," I said. "I just want to talk to her about the boat that went missing. It might not even be related to the map at all."

As the words came out of my mouth, I prayed I was wrong. I hoped the missing boat had everything to do with the map.

***

When the bell rang that afternoon, I waited for Shelby by the front doors of the school. As usual, she was late, and I became impatient waiting for her. I debated taking out my cell phone and texting her, but there was a strict no-texting rule in the school and since I was standing right outside the office, I decided to follow the rules.

"I'm here, I'm here," announced Shelby. "I know you're upset, but I'm not that late."

"You're *twenty minutes* late! What were you doing?"

"I was trying to explain to Jimmy Carson why he is such a jerk. He didn't seem to understand so I had to tell him a few times."

I suspected that she had a crush on Jimmy, but it would probably be a while before she admitted it.

"Can we go now?" I asked.

Shelby opened the door and we left the school in search of Maggie Gordon's house.

***

"How much further is it?" Shelby asked, breathless after having walked almost fifteen minutes.

"Farther," I corrected. "And not much. Just a little bit more."

I'd printed a map before we left the house, showing the best route to take from the school to Maggie's house. According to the map, we were only one street away.

"What are you going to say when you get there?" Shelby asked.

"I'm not sure. I'll figure it out when she answers the door." I stopped on the sidewalk, and grabbed Shelby by the arm. "But please don't try to help me. Just stay quiet."

Shelby rolled her eyes and muttered, "Whatever."

We soon found ourselves outside of Maggie Gordon's house. It was a nice, but simple house. It was not very big, and did not stand out in any way from the rest of the houses on the street.

"Well we know one thing," Shelby began. "She

clearly doesn't have the missing gold, this place is a dump."

This was exactly the type of comment I thought Shelby might make in front of Maggie, and it made me terribly nervous. I began to question my judgment and asked myself why I hadn't brought Tricia instead.

I rang the bell and Shelby tapped her foot impatiently on the porch beneath us.

"Can you stop that?" I said. "You're making me nervous."

The front door opened and an elderly woman with a cane stood before us.

"Hello," she said. "Can I help you?"

"Hi. Are you Maggie Gordon?"

"Yes, I am."

A part of me had hoped she wasn't Maggie Gordon, and that we had the wrong house entirely. That, unfortunately, was not the case. I needed to start thinking on my feet, and fast.

"I'm Cora Flash... and I am doing a school project about the boat your husband was on. The one that went missing."

"Oh," she said after a long pause. "I see."

Her expression suddenly turned very sad; she was clearly still heartbroken at the loss of her husband.

"You should come in, then." She held open the door.

We walked into her house and sat ourselves in her living room. It reminded me of my grandmother's house— very dark with lots of wood, carpet and pillows.

"It smells like soup in here," Shelby said to me. Thankfully, she was very discreet when she said it.

"So," said Maggie, "you're doing a project on the S.S. Guppy, are you?"

Although this was not entirely accurate, I decided it was mostly true since my school project had led me to the story of the missing boat in the first place.

"That's right," I said. "And I wanted to ask you a few questions about the day your husband's boat went missing. I read an article from when it happened, but I thought you might know more about it."

"I probably don't," she said. "Most of what we learned about the boat was what we read in the newspapers. We were never told what really happened, or if the boat turned up somewhere else."

"So you've never heard from your husband?" I

asked.

"No, bless him. Lyle would have said something, he would have sent a letter or a postcard to tell me he was okay."

"What do you think happened?" asked Shelby.

"I believe the ship sank in stormy weather. It had a large cargo of gold, which you can imagine is very heavy. If a boat loaded with tons of gold bars starts to take on water, it is going to sink very quickly."

She was probably right. I tried to picture the boat with water pouring in from the river, and all of the gold adding to the weight of the ship. It would have sunk very fast.

"Unfortunately," continued Maggie, "most everyone else thinks the crew of the ship made off with the cargo, and they sailed out to South America or some other part of the world and are living like kings with the stolen gold."

"Did you ever believe that?" I asked.

"Not for a second," she replied. "Not my Lyle. My Lyle was a good man. He was an honest man. He would never steal anything, even if his life depended on it."

"You must miss him," I said.

I looked at Maggie's face and could see a small

tear forming in her eye. "Terribly," she said. "The worst thing is not knowing what happened. And because we never found out, the insurance company refuses to pay any of the life insurance we had taken out. So I have been living very carefully my entire life, but have almost lost this house on more than one occasion. This house is all I have left of Lyle, and I cannot bear the thought of losing it."

Maggie's face softened as the pleasant memories of her days with Lyle came back.

"When we were first married, we didn't have much money. Lyle was working such long hours on the ships, but not making much. He managed all of our finances, so I never knew exactly how much money we had. There was always enough for groceries and our rent, but not much more. Well, it turned out that Lyle was putting away a little money each month, and after three years of marriage, he surprised me with this house. He said it was the wedding present he couldn't afford to give me when we were first married."

"Oh," said Shelby, practically on the verge of tears. "That's so sweet."

"He was a very sweet man, and I can still picture him walking through that door and sitting down in that chair," she said, pointing to a chair in the corner. "This house is all I have left of him."

I thanked Maggie for her time and asked if I could return if I had any more questions. She graciously agreed and told me I could come back as often as I wanted.

Outside the house, I looked at Shelby and said, "We have to find out what happened to Lyle. That poor woman can't live the rest of her life thinking her husband is a crook."

FOURTEEN

Saturday morning, I gathered my bag of supplies for the day, making sure to include my binoculars, camera and a couple of snacks. Sailing always made me hungry.

Thankfully, Tricia called to tell me her dad was okay with Calvin coming along. I'd never taken Calvin sailing before, but I imagined the wind blowing through his fur would be a great thrill for him. And he seemed to appreciate any opportunity to get out of the house.

"Cora!" Mom called from down the hall. "Mr.

Morgan is here!"

I looked out my bedroom window to see Tricia's dad leaning over the car, washing the windows with a spray bottle and cloth. Tricia said ever since he bought the new car, only a few weeks prior, he was obsessed with cleaning the windows.

"It's like he can't see through the window unless it's completely spotless," she complained one day during lunch.

I zipped up my bag and threw it over my shoulder.

"Come on," I said to Calvin, who had been snoozing on the bed.

Calvin jumped off the bed and ran straight to the front door. He knew we were going out, but I couldn't wait for him to find out where.

"Do you have everything?" Mom asked.

"I think so. I brought a change of clothes just in case I get wet."

"Good thinking."

The last time I sailed with Tricia and her father, I slipped off the boat as we boarded and fell right into the river. Having fallen right next to the dock I could easily scramble out, and was never in any danger but boy did I know what it felt like to be embarrassed.

"Try not to fall," said Mom, with only a slight hint of genuine concern. She knew I would be fine.

"I won't. Okay, see you!"

I kissed her goodbye and waved to Ethan, who was rolling around on the floor of the living room, laughing to himself.

Grabbing Calvin's leash, I opened the door and ran out to Mr. Morgan's new car.

"Hi, Cora!" he said, fanatically scrubbing away a spot on his windshield only he could see.

"Hi! Thanks for inviting me. I always love sailing."

"We're glad to have you along," he said, finally pleased with his windshield cleaning efforts.

Calvin jumped in the back seat and settled down next to me as I said hello to Tricia in the front seat.

"Where's Shelby?" I asked.

"She's going to meet us there," replied Tricia. "She has a dance lesson, so she's going straight to the dock."

Shelby thought of herself as quite a dancer, even though she was as graceful as a door falling off its hinges. I didn't dare tell her that.

"I brought my camera so I could take lots of pictures for a school project," I said to Mr. Morgan.

"I'll make sure I don't go too fast so you can get

some great shots."

***

The Morgans' boat was the biggest sailboat I'd ever been on, but was certainly not the biggest boat in the marina. Many others towered over the Morgans' boat. Some of them even had a crew of several people to manage everything. Mr. Morgan was able to control his boat mostly on his own, but occasionally would ask us to pull a rope or hold the steering wheel for a bit while he adjusted one of the sails.

When we pulled up to the marina, Shelby and her mother were already waiting for us. We exchanged hellos before boarding the boat.

"Just so you know, I painted my nails this morning, so I am not going to be able to help with any of the sailing... stuff," Shelby announced. "I don't want to chip a nail"

The water that day was particularly smooth and the sky couldn't have been any clearer; A perfect day for taking photos.

"My book said that this was one of the busiest shipping lanes in the region," I said to Shelby and Tricia. "Ten or twenty boats a day would pass through here with their cargo."

"Wow," said Shelby dryly. "Sounds exciting."

"Well I think it's very exciting," said Tricia. "We don't have to do that project in my class, but I wish we did."

"You could do mine," said Shelby. "No one has to know."

"Shelby," boomed Mr. Morgan from the helm of the boat. "You know I can hear you."

"I was just kidding," she replied, although we all knew she'd been very serious.

I took out my camera and started to take pictures of the surroundings. I tried to imagine what it would have been like with cargo boats full of goods making their way downriver.

"What happened when all of the industry moved away?" I asked Mr. Morgan. "Where did the people go?"

"They left town, I guess," he said. "People go where the jobs are. Like your dad. He's on the road traveling because that's where his business is. If he could, I'm sure he would rather be in town working here with you and your mom and Ethan close by."

Calvin had found himself a small bench to sit on, but faced out to the river, watching the other boats and birds go by.

"Having a good day little guy?" I asked.

He looked at me and through his wind-blown

fur, I swear he was smiling.

As I resumed taking pictures for my project, I noticed a huge cliff face come into view. It was what we called Beggar's Bluff. Beggar's Bluff was a large cliff face that jutted out over the river. Some people went there to climb, but often found themselves landing in the river after failing to scale the very steep rock face. I had only seen it from the water, but had never gone there in person. My parents always told me to stay away; they said it was far too dangerous.

"I don't want to get too close to the bluffs," said Mr. Morgan, "but I thought you would want to take a few pictures for your project."

He was right; I knew my pictures would be a great addition to the project.

I must have snapped a dozen pictures when something in my head clicked. I suddenly realized I had to take a look at the map I'd brought.

Putting the camera down, I reached for my bag and pulled out the treasure map and studied it. The jagged drawing by the water with the big red 'X' in the map became instantly recognizable. Beggar's Bluff!

The treasure in this map must be at Beggar's Bluff!

FIFTEEN

"Is that it?" asked Shelby, pointing to the map in my hand, the one with the big red X that no doubt would lead to millions of dollars in jewels and money. She had surprised me by sneaking up while I sat on a bench outside the school Wednesday morning.

"Yes." I said.

"Shelby told me about it," said Tricia. "Where did you get it?"

I was not in the least surprised to hear Shelby had told Tricia about the map, even though I was planning to keep it to myself.

"I found it in a book I'm using for my project."

Tricia leaned in for a closer look. "It's definitely a treasure map."

"How delightful!" exclaimed Shelby. "I wonder what kind of treasure it leads to?"

"I don't know. I'm not even sure it's real."

"I think it is!" said Shelby. "I have seen treasure maps before, and this looks just like one."

"Where have you seen one before?" asked Tricia.

"In movies, tons of them. My brother watches pirate movies all the time, and this is what the treasure maps look like. Oh, I wonder what the treasure is going to be. Gold coins, probably, and maybe even some rubies or emeralds."

"Don't get carried away," I said.

"Oh," continued Shelby, not paying any attention to me, "I hope it's not booby-trapped. I've seen some of the movies where they have spears and guns that shoot you when you try to walk by! That would be horrible!"

Yes, it certainly would.

"Aarrf!" exclaimed Calvin.

I looked at my dog, who was eyeing Beggar's Bluff. He knew there was something interesting about that formation, and I could not agree with him more.

Clearly, the map indicated that formation as the spot with the X. It had to be the place with the treasure, but what was the treasure?

"Mr. Morgan," I said. "Can we stop for a bit so I can take a few pictures?"

"I can't really stop," he replied, "but I can slow down and we can stay in this area. Come on up where I am, you'll get a much better view."

I climbed up to the hull where Mr. Morgan had been steering and he was right, I could see for miles.

Although I wasn't exactly sure what I was taking pictures of, I snapped as many as I could so I could study the cliffs later at home.

A loud horn signaled from behind us, alarming everyone except Mr. Morgan who seemed to find the noise a welcome distraction.

We looked to where the sound had come from and recognized the vessel right away. Gerald Pape on his fishing boat, out for his usual day of work and passing us on the starboard side.

"Ahoy!" yelled Mr. Morgan. I had the feeling that sailor speak made him very happy.

"Ahoy Jake! Hi girls!" Gerald yelled to us, waving his arms.

We all yelled hello back as Gerald passed us in the choppy water. Even Calvin let out a few yelps.

After Gerald's boat passed, Mr. Morgan suggested we take a little lunch break. He had thoughtfully packed a picnic lunch with an assortment of sandwiches and cut-up pieces of pineapple, my favorite! He'd even brought along some organic dog treats for Calvin. Calvin hated to be left out, particularly where food was involved.

I knew my mom would be out at the mall with Ethan when we returned home, so I asked Mr. Morgan if he would drive me home. As usual, he was happy to help.

"I hope your pictures turn out," he said as we arrived at my house.

"I'm sure they will." I had no doubt the pictures would turn out, but I was more concerned about what they would reveal when I studied them for more clues about the treasure.

"Thank you for the ride," I said as I exited the car. "I'll call you later, Tricia."

"Bye!" she said, waving from the front seat.

"Come on Calvin, let's go."

***

When I got back to my room, I immediately

connected my camera to my computer and clicked "download." A small icon appeared on the screen and showed my pictures flying through the air and into a folder on my desktop. After a few minutes, the files were transferred, and I was ready to start examining them.

The first bunch showed the water and the boat, as well as a couple of goofy poses of me, Shelby, Tricia and Calvin. Mr. Morgan could be seen in the background laughing at the four of us.

When I got to the pictures of Beggar's Bluff, I double clicked on the first one to make it full screen. I did not see anything unusual about the very steep cliff face, with many jagged rocks sticking out in all directions. No wonder people got hurt trying to climb it.

I felt like I was looking for a needle in a haystack, without knowing what a needle even looked like. To me, it just looked like a cliff. I could not imagine where any treasure might be hidden.

After looking through all of my pictures, I printed off a few of them in a size small enough for me to carry around in my bag, next to the half torn treasure map. If I discovered something else later, I would have the pictures at my disposal to study.

As I replaced my bag, I saw Calvin with his nose

buried under my dresser, trying to root out something. I am not supposed to eat in my room, but sometimes I sneak something in and occasionally a piece will fall off and roll under my bed or the dresser. Calvin will usually find it pretty quickly and cry until I reach under and pull it out. Knowing he would not give up until I gave in, I reached under the dresser and started feeling around for whatever it was that Calvin was after.

It was not food that Calvin had discovered, it seemed, but some sort of card. A library card. Not a regular card, however; it had a big 'S' on it, right beside the barcode with no signature or name on it. Whoever broke into my room had left a very valuable piece of evidence behind.

"Calvin," I said. "You have just sniffed out a very important clue!"

SIXTEEN

As much as I wanted to bring him with me, I knew Calvin would not be allowed in the library, and I couldn't leave him tied up outside while I investigated.

I hopped on my bike and rode as fast as I could to the library, determined to find out who owned the card I'd found on my bedroom floor.

***

Mr. Burton, the librarian, was not at the front desk when I went in. This disappointed me, as I found him very helpful and would no doubt have looked up the name of the person who had dropped their card. The bigger disappointment was that in his place stood Marty Bass. Marty Bass happened to be the seventeen-year-old brother of Alex Bass, my classmate. Marty worked part-time in the library, but did not actually seem to do much work.

"Hi, Marty," I said. "Where's Mr. Burton?"

"Oh, hey Cora," he said, sounding half-asleep. "He's at lunch right now. He should be back in, like, ten or fifteen minutes."

"Maybe you can help me," I said, taking out the card from my pocket. "I found this and I wanted to return it to its owner. Can you tell me who it belongs to?"

He looked at the card and narrowed his eyes.

"You found this?" he said.

"Yes."

"Where?"

I began to fear Marty suspected something about the card, so I decided to lie in order to keep him from asking more questions. "I found it in the street."

"Oh," he replied. "It's just that... this is not a regular library card. You see the big 'S' on it? That stands for 'Staff'. This card belongs to a staff member."

"Are you sure?"

"I'm sure," he said. "Look."

He rifled through his wallet and took out his own library card, which looked just like the one I had found.

"Can you tell who this card belongs to?"

"Yeah, but there are only a few people this could belong to. I know it's not mine, but could be one of the other students who work here."

He took the card and punched the number into the computer and waited a second.

"It's Mr. Burton's card. He must have dropped it."

A horrible thought passed through my head. Mr. Burton could not have been the person to break into my house, could he? Was he the person who was trying to find the other half of the map?

"Marty, do you know if Mr. Burton lost his wallet lately?"

I thought perhaps the thief had stolen Mr. Burton's wallet and dropped the card in my bedroom.

"No," replied Marty. "He never mentioned it. In fact, I noticed he had his wallet with him this morning. He took it out and started looking through it. Come to think of it, he looked like he was looking for something, probably his card."

"Thanks Marty, but do me a favor. Don't tell him I have the card. I want to give it to him myself. I want to surprise him."

"Sure, no problem."

I knew it would be a big surprise when I showed the card to Mr. Burton, so I had to make sure it was at the right moment, but first I had something else to do.

I had to find the other half of the treasure map before Mr. Burton came back from lunch.

SEVENTEEN

The library office was at the back of the building, in a secluded corner. I had seen Mr. Burton go in it a hundred times, enough to notice he did not lock it.

I slowly walked to the back of the library, making sure no one was paying very much attention to me as I made my way to the office. Luckily, there were not many people in the book stacks at the far corner of the room, so I was easily able to sneak into the office without being noticed.

Marty had said Mr. Burton would be back in ten

minutes, so I had to act fast.

The office was very well organized with a large desk and a small filing cabinet next to it, which seemed to suit a librarian well. Aside from that, stacks and stacks of boxes filled with books lined every wall of the office.

As I started to rifle through the desk drawer, I remembered my friend Abby and me doing the same thing in Mount Topaz—searching for clues in Preston Thurgood's office about the supposedly haunted hotel!

The top drawer had only pens, pencils and other stuff you'd need in an office. No treasure maps, however. I started to look through the drawers one by one. The first one only had food in it: Granola bars, fruit rolls and toaster pastries. It was a wonder Mr. Burton left for lunch at all; He could survive on the food in his desk for several days.

The other desk drawers did not turn up anything of interest. I decided to move onto the cabinet.

Working quickly, I dug through the files to see if anything caught my eye. They appeared to be invoices from different publishers and book distributors— all somehow related to the business of running a library. Not interesting.

I sat back in Mr. Burton's chair and looked up at

the ceiling, preparing to admit the map was not in his office. I noticed one of the ceiling tiles pushed up slightly at one corner. On a hunch, I decided to check it out.

I quickly scrambled on top of Mr. Burton's desk and pushed the ceiling tile up. The corner of a piece of paper stuck out from the tile beside the one I was lifting.

"Ah-ha. What's this?"

I took out the piece of paper and unfolded it. The other half of the treasure map!

Mr. Burton would be back any second. I quickly jumped down from the desk and ran to the small five-in-one printer/fax machine in the corner of his office. I put the map down on the glass screen and pressed 'COPY'.

The copy machine whirred as it warmed up and began to scan, then print, a copy. It felt like it took forever, and I was convinced Mr. Burton would walk in on me.

As soon as the copier spat out my paper, I grabbed the original off the glass and folded it back up as I had found it. As quick as I had taken it, I replaced it back above the ceiling tile.

I folded up my copy and stuffed it in my jeans pocket, right beside the library card with the 'S' on it.

As I exited the office, I could see Mr. Burton enter the library from the front doors. Luckily, I was too far back in the building for him to see me, so I was able to walk up to the front without raising any suspicions.

"Cora," Mr. Burton said. "Back again? You've been quite a regular here. Did you find what you needed?"

"Yes," I replied. "I found *exactly* what I needed."

I walked out the front door and turned to look at Marty, who still stood behind the desk. After making sure Mr. Burton could not see me, I put my index finger up to my lips and winked at Marty, discretely making a "Shhh" sound that only he would notice.

EIGHTEEN

No doubt about it, the map I had found in the office was the other half of the map I had found tucked into the book.

As soon as I got home, I pulled out my half of the map and put it together with the one I'd copied from Mr. Burton's office. The picture started to make sense. The river that wound through the map curved up at the top, just like the river in town. Buildings drawn on the map were obviously the buildings that would have existed at the time the maps were drawn. The Bank, the old brick storefronts on Main Street, it was all there on the other half of the map.

The most interesting part was written at the top. Words at the left side of the map read "THE TH" and "MEN KN" underneath. When I put the new part of the map beside the half I had found, I could read the whole message.

"THE THREE WISE MEN KNOW ALL."

I read it to myself a few times, not knowing exactly what it meant. Who were the three wise men? I know of the three wise men in the bible, but what did that have to do with the treasure? Who were they and where could I find them?

My mind shifted back to Mr. Burton. I couldn't believe I'd found his library card in my room. He had the other half of the map, so it made sense that he would want to find my half, but it had been in the library the whole time! He could have found it any time he wanted... unless he hadn't known where to look.

"Bling!"

My computer announced an incoming video chat from Tricia.

"Hi Tricia," I said.

"Hi Cora. Any more luck with the treasure map? Did you figure it out?"

"Sort of, but I'm not sure of something."

I held up the two pieces of the map side by side so she could see the complete picture.

"There is a reference to the three wise men, I'm not sure what it means."

"The three wise men know all," read Tricia. "It's from the bible."

"I know that," I said, "but what does it have to do with this?"

"I'm not sure, but I know you'll figure it out. Hey, where did you find the other half of the map?"

I debated telling her what I'd done. She might not approve of my breaking into Mr. Burton's office to look for the map. If it had been Shelby, there would have been no problem at all.

"I found it," I finally said.

"Where?" she pressed.

After a few seconds, I replied with an answer that was, basically, true. "In the library."

"In another book?"

"No, I found it in Mr. Burton's office."

"Why was it in Mr. Burton's office?"

I decided to let her in on my secret, even if she judged me.

"I found something..." I began.

"Aarf!" Calvin interrupted.

"Sorry," I said. "Calvin found something that led me to believe Mr. Burton was the person who broke into my house."

"Mr. Burton? Cora, don't be ridiculous. Librarians don't break into houses."

"He dropped his library card in my room, it was under the dresser. Marty Bass looked it up and confirmed it was Mr. Burton's card."

"So you figured he must have had the other half of the map so you broke into his office to find it? Wow, that's crazy, Cora."

She was right; it was crazy, and dangerous.

"Do you think he knows you know?"

I hadn't even considered that, and the thought made me very nervous.

"I don't know. I don't think so, but maybe he still hasn't discovered he dropped his card. And I doubt he will realize he dropped it here."

"Just be careful, Cora, and you should tell your mom."

I knew she was right, but if I told my Mom, I'd never get a chance to search for the missing treasure. I had to hold out for just a few more days.

"Are you busy tomorrow?" I asked.

"No, why?"

"I'm going to need your help. We have to figure

out what the three wise men have to do with this."

NINETEEN

"We're probably going to deny all of the claims in the bus accident case," my mother announced.

We had just finished eating breakfast on Sunday morning and were sitting at the table talking about her insurance case.

"I went to visit the Doctor who signed the medical forms for three of the people involved in the case and you'll never guess what I found out."

"What?"

My mom had a very excited look on her face. "The doctor has never heard of any of them! Their claims were falsified; they made everything up, including the signature on the forms. I compared it to the doctor's real signature and they are nothing alike! Next I'm going to start looking into the other claims and see if there is a similar situation, but it appears as though everyone on the bus was in on this together, I just have to prove they know each other somehow."

"When are you going to talk to the other people?"

"Today, and I'll need your help. Remember when I took this job I said I would need your help with Ethan from time to time?"

I could feel the hairs on the back of my neck standing up. I did not like where the conversation was going.

"Yeah..." I said.

"I need your help today. I need you to watch Ethan for a few hours while I conduct a few more interviews."

I was crushed. I had planned to do more work on *my* case, and this would change everything. Unless....

"Can I bring Ethan with me while I work on my project? I have to talk to Mr. French at the town hall."

"Of course," my mom said. "Just be careful. He's been a bit of a daredevil lately."

My mom was absolutely right. Ethan had only been on his feet a short time, but had quickly progressed from walking to sprinting. He would disappear the minute you turned your head. I had my work cut out for me.

"I'll be extra careful," I said.

This made my mom happy. Her face relaxed a little bit.

"Thank you," she said. "You know how much this means to me."

TWENTY

Since Ethan was such a slow walker, I decided to put him in his stroller to keep us moving at a decent pace. I tied Calvin's leash to the stroller to make sure he kept up with us as well.

The Town Hall was one of the tallest buildings in our town, but that is not saying very much. It was only tall because of the large dome that stood on the top of the roof. When I was really little, I used to think that the mayor lived in the dome. I later learned this was not, in fact, true and that it was actually empty up there; it was just a façade.

Once inside the town hall, it was not hard to find the "museum," housed entirely in a glass case at the back of the room.

I pushed the stroller to the glass case and told Ethan and Calvin to stay put. There was no one around so I started to examine the contents: a bunch of photos, mostly from the twenties and thirties, of the old storefronts and people who used to live in the town; a picture of a big fat guy with a big necklace around his neck, the kind a mayor would wear. It did not take much to deduce that he was, probably, the mayor at the time.

Next to the photos sat a large piece of rock, smooth on two sides.

"That's a brick, or what's left of one," said a voice.

I spun around to see Mr. French behind me. He had a full head of grey hair, cut very short, and wore a button up shirt and nice dress pants. He took pride in the way he dressed and from his smile, he was obviously pleased someone had taken an interest in local history.

"A brick?"

"Yes," he explained. "From the original town hall, which burned down in the 1940s. This one was built to replace it, and we kept one of the bricks to remember the building that stood here."

"Oh," I said. "Did you live here at the time?"

I did not want to risk insulting him, but he looked to be in his seventies, so I knew it was a reasonable shot that he may have been alive.

"Yes, but I was just a boy. I remember the fire, though. It was terrible. We didn't have modern fire pumpers like we have today, we only had men with hand pumped water hoses. I don't think that old building stood a chance, being mostly made of wood."

"Was anyone hurt?"

"I don't think so. Not from what I recall, but my parents would not have said as much, I suppose. I do remember that there was talk it had been arson, but I don't think they ever got to the bottom of it."

"What a terrible thing for someone to do," I said.

"Aarf!" interrupted Calvin, reminding me to get to the reason we were here.

"Oh," I said. "Do you know anything about the boat that went missing?"

"You mean the S.S. Guppy? Why, yes, of course. It was full of gold bars from upriver. Went missing on its way out of town."

"Do you know what happened to it?"

"There were rumors that the crew hijacked the boat and took off with the gold. People said they were probably living the lives of kings somewhere in South America, but I can't see that at all. My family knew a few of the sailors on that boat, and I can't see them doing anything like that. They were good, upstanding citizens. They didn't have enough greed in their system to attempt something like that."

As much as Mr. French's character witness said of his belief in the sailors, I could not discount the possibility that the rumors were true. I had to keep it under consideration.

I decided to switch gears and ask about the treasure map, but not in an obvious way.

"What do you know about the Three Wise Men?" I asked.

"You mean from the bible?"

"No, I mean around here. Is there something around here called the Three Wise Men?"

"Oh! Of course, I should have guessed. The Three Wise Men are over in Beggar's Bluff. It's a formation of three rocks, side by side, that people always thought looked like three men with crowns on, so they nicknamed them the Three Wise Men. It's way over on the other side of the bluffs, but the water is so choppy and dangerous on that side that most people avoid it."

It was all making sense now. The map pointed to Beggar's Bluff, and the clue said "THE THREE WISE MEN KNOW ALL." That probably meant that the treasure was somewhere near the Three Wise Men.

"Can anyone get there by land?" I asked, imagining myself pushing the stroller and dragging Calvin all the way to the cliffs.

"Oh, good gracious no," he said. "There is no way to get there by land, only by boat. And you have to be a very experienced sailor to get there."

I only knew two experienced sailors, and one of them was Tricia's father. I doubted he would be willing to take me there, at least not without asking permission from my mother. Permission that she would never give. The other was Gerald Pape. I had to ask Gerald to take me to the Three Wise Men.

TWENTY-ONE

Later that afternoon, I video chatted with both Shelby and Tricia. I would need all the support I could get from them when I went to Beggar's Bluff.

"No way, not a chance," said Shelby. "That is too dangerous, Cora. You'll get us all killed."

"I hate to agree with Shelby," Tricia added. That was true, she *hated* to agree with Shelby. "My Dad won't even sail there, he said it probably caused at least a hundred shipwrecks."

I was so disappointed in both of them. I thought they would be really excited when I asked them to come.

"It's a treasure hunt!" I yelled.

"Still no," said Shelby.

"Sorry, Cora," said Tricia.

"I think you're both overreacting," I pleaded. "Boats today are capable of sailing in very dangerous waters now, it will be fine."

Despite my plea, both girls declined to join me on my adventure, even after promising we would return at the first sign of trouble.

"Well, Calvin," I said. "Looks like it's just the two of us."

"Blurg!" yelled Ethan, who was in the hallway smashing two of his expensive toys together.

"Oh, right. Just the three of us."

I arrived at Gerald Pape's boat slip with Ethan and Calvin just as he was handing off his catch of the day to one of his customers.

"Thanks Gerald, this looks great," said the appreciative customer.

"See ya tomorrow," he said.

When the other man left, I stepped up to the boat, taking his place.

"Hi Gerald."

"Oh hi, Cora," he replied. "And Ethan too.

What brings you guys here?"

"I have a favor to ask of you."

I knew this was going to be hard sell.

"I have a school project that I am working on, and I really need to take some photos, up close photos, of Beggar's Bluff, and I was hoping you would take me."

Gerald's expression turned to one of confusion. "But I saw you taking pictures out there on the Morgan boat just yesterday."

I knew I would have to tell a tiny lie to get Gerald to agree to take me out on his boat.

"They didn't turn out. I got home and checked the camera and they were all blank. And my presentation is due soon, so I really need to get the pictures."

Gerald considered my request and finally agreed to take me to Beggar's Bluff.

"All right," he said. "I'll take you. I got in a little early today, so I have some time to spare. But we'll have to get going right away before it gets dark, and you can't bring that onboard."

He was pointing to Ethan's stroller. I would have to leave it on the dock and take Ethan with me.

"Fine," I said. "I can just leave it here."

We climbed on board the boat and sat down at the front.

I knew there was only a short period of time before I confessed to Gerald about my true intentions. It wouldn't be long before he realized I didn't even have my camera with me!

TWENTY-TWO

We followed the same route that we'd taken with Tricia's father for the first part of the trip, but headed out much farther from shore than Mr. Morgan had.

"I can't believe I let you talk me into this," said Gerald. "Your mother is going to kill me!"

Shortly after we left the dock, I decided to tell him the real reason for my wanting to go to Beggar's Bluff. I knew if I did not confess early on, there would be no way he would be convinced to continue the trip.

"It will be worth it," I said. "Don't worry."

We rode through the waves, which began to crash higher and higher against the side of the boat the closer we came to Beggar's Bluff.

"I think the Three Wise Men are just around the other side," Gerald said.

I looked at Ethan, who was sitting in the seat beside me, bundled up in a lifejacket. Calvin sat on top of his seat, looking out at the bluffs. I could tell he couldn't wait to get there and start exploring.

After cruising for nearly forty minutes in the direction of the red X, it was beginning to look like we would *never* find the spot where the treasure was.

"Cora," said Gerald from the wheelhouse. "I don't know if we're going to find anything, I don't see anything around here. It's all just rocks."

He was right; everywhere we looked was rocks and water—no signs of anything that might lead to treasure.

"We have to just keep going for a little bit longer," I pleaded.

Gerald shook his head in doubt, but agreed to keep going, but only for a short while.

The boat puttered along, with Calvin and me keeping watch for anything that might look out of the ordinary. I was beginning to lose faith, and wondered if I had not read the map correctly. I pulled it out of my pocket and looked at it again.

Impossible, I thought to myself. *It has to be here.*

No other place fit the map as well as Beggar's Bluff, but I was beginning to think I was wrong. I joined Gerald in the wheelhouse to tell him we should turn back.

"I'm sorry I led you on a wild goose chase," I said to him. "I must have read it wrong."

Gerald looked down at me and tried his best to console me. "Oh, Cora," he said. "I'm sure you'll figure it out. If the treasure is not here, then I'm sure you'll figure out where it is."

"I guess so," I said, crushed. "We can go back now."

"All right then," Gerald said. "Let's turn her around."

He started to turn the big steering wheel of his boat to begin our trip back to shore.

Just as the boat started to turn, Calvin spotted something and started barking ferociously—almost as intensely as when he encountered a squirrel in the park.

"What is it, Calvin?"

He continued to bark, staring straight ahead at a rock formation. I looked at the formation that had caught Calvin's attention. Three large rocks jutted out of the water at least fifty feet in the air! I had never seen them before, I was sure of it.

"Gerald!" I yelled. "Look ahead. What is that?"

Gerald squinted his eyes, trying to make out what was in front of us. "I don't know, Cora. Let's bring her in a little closer."

Gerald started to steer the boat back over to the rock formation Calvin had been barking at. The rocks grew larger and larger the closer we got to them. I could see where people thought it looked like three men with crowns on, but if I hadn't been told first, I don't think I would have arrived at the same conclusion. I thought it looked much more like three beer bottles with the caps on upside down.

"This must be it!" I yelled.

Gerald slowed the engine down, as we were getting very close to the jagged rocks surrounding the Three Wise Men.

"I don't know how close I can get," he said. "The water is rough and the rocks are very jagged, it's too dangerous."

"Try to get a bit closer," I pleaded.

I could barely see anything around the Three Wise Men that might lead to the treasure, but there had to be something here, the map said so.

"Arr, arr!" yelped Calvin.

He stared at a spot just behind the rocks. A small cave that went into the bluffs directly behind the Three Wise Men. That had to be it!

"Gerald, we have to go in there!" I yelled.

Gerald, who could easily have argued with me, decided it was worth checking out. He expertly steered his fishing boat into the cave that Calvin had spotted. Soon after entering the cave, we realized none of us could see for the darkness.

"We'll have to turn on the light," said Gerald, his words echoing all around us.

He turned on the spotlight affixed to the roof of the wheelhouse on his boat. The light flooded the cave, which was more of a cavern. The water continued into the cave, which must have been one hundred feet high. The rock formations that climbed the walls and hung from the ceilings gave eerie shadows as the light hit them. It was very spooky, and overwhelming.

"Cora," said Gerald, "something's up ahead. Can you tell what it is?"

I made my way to the front of the boat and saw a dark shadow in front of us.

"We're too far from it, I can't tell what it is."

Gerald moved us closer, the light filling more

and more of the cavern as we puttered along. Soon, the light lit up the dark mass in front of us. One of the first things I was able to read were the letters, "S.S. Guppy."

TWENTY-THREE

As we moved closer, more and more of the boat became visible. Clearly, this was the final resting place of the S.S. Guppy. It was badly beaten up, the front of the boat was smashed in and resting on a flat rocky stretch of the cavern.

"They must have hit a bad storm," said Gerald, as he focused the light on the wreckage. "And thought this cavern would provide some refuge."

Gerald cut the motor of his boat and anchored us beside a flat rock that would allow us to climb out of the boat to explore where the S.S. Guppy had landed.

"Hold my hand!" I sternly instructed Ethan. He gripped it tightly. He was probably too scared to go anywhere, but I had to make sure he stayed with me.

Calvin ran happily ahead of us, off-leash. There were not many places for him to go, so I figured he would appreciate the freedom of not being tied to me.

"Be careful where you step," said Gerald. "It's slippery here."

Gerald left the boat's searchlight on so we would be able to see where we were going.

"Take this, just in case," he added, handing me a flashlight.

We slowly made our way toward the wreckage. Clearly beyond repair, the boat had either crashed into some rocks outside of the bluffs or made its way here, or else crashed into the rocks inside the cavern as they tried to slow down. Without a light like the one Gerald had, it would have been nearly impossible to safely slow the boat down in time to properly dock.

Calvin had run ahead of us, busily exploring a battered up old blanket. He sniffed it with great excitement and pawed at it, trying to move it.

"What have you found there, buddy?" I asked.

I kneeled down in front of the blanket, which looked like a tarp. It must have been a covering for something on the boat, but covered up whatever Calvin had discovered.

Gerald stood beside me with his flashlight pointed at the object Calvin had discovered, so I was able to put mine down. As I was still holding on to Ethan, I pulled the tarp off with my one free hand.

Gerald and I both gasped.

Under the tarp was a pile of fifty or sixty bars of gold.

"Well, I'll be...," said Gerald. "Will you look at that?"

"Is this all of it?" I asked aloud.

"Probably not," he answered. "These boats can hold much more than this, but maybe this is all the crew could get out safely."

I picked up one of the bars. It was not shiny like I'd expected it to be but, given that we'd found it in a cave after it had been lost for decades, I guessed that was normal. It was extremely heavy, though, and I was shocked at how much it weighed.

"I need to pick one up," said Gerald, bending down to grab a bar from the pile.

He held it in both hands, bouncing it up and

down to feel the weight of it. His eyes were wide with excitement, clearly enjoying our discovery!

As we stared at the gold, I could hear Calving batting something around behind the pile. Then I heard a clinking sound, like the sound of ice cubes in a glass.

Calvin appeared from behind the pile of gold with a bottle in his mouth! The sound I'd heard was his teeth closing around the stem of the bottle.

"What is that?" I asked, taking it from his mouth.

A small cork plugged up the top of the bottle, which contained a rolled-up piece of paper.

"Maybe it's a letter," I said, removing the cork.

The paper was jammed in the bottle; I couldn't get it out. I was about to smash the bottle on the rocks when I had a better idea.

"Ethan," I said. "Get it out!"

I knew Ethan's tiny baby fingers would be able to reach into the top of the bottle a little easier than mine. I was right, Ethan removed the letter from the bottle easily. He handed me the paper, but kept the bottle.

Unrolling the letter, I could see it was a handwritten note of some kind. I read the note out so Gerald could hear.

"Dear Maggie," I began. The letter must have been written by Lyle! *"No doubt you have heard by now of our ship being lost at sea. We hit a terrible storm just after we passed town and have been here in this cavern for five days since our boat crashed. We took refuge in this cavern, hoping we would be able to sail back out and continue on our journey, but the waves were too rough and we smashed the hull of the boat as we came into the bluffs. We have no radio and no search party has come close enough for us to try and signal. A few of the crew, myself included, are going to try and sail out on a makeshift boat tomorrow morning, but I do not know what fate has in store, but if you should not hear from me, please remember I will always love you. XO, Lyle."*

It was such a sad letter to read. Lyle and the other crew members must have known they were heading into such terrible danger as they tried to escape the cavern. He'd left this note for someone to discover in case he did not make it back to town.

"They must have been lost at sea," said Gerald. "Their boat never made it back."

This made me very sad, but I was happy that Maggie would be able to rest knowing her husband was not part of a band of gold thieves.

"One of the other crew members must have made the map," I said. "They probably threw that one in the water and it made its way back to civilization."

"Right you are!" said a voice from behind us.

Gerald, Ethan, Calvin and I all turned around, startled.

There stood Mr. Burton, the Librarian and house burglar, pointing a gun right at us.

"You're not the only one with a boat!" he said.

TWENTY-FOUR

"What in blazes are you doing, Frank?" said Gerald. "Put that thing away."

"Mind your business, Gerald. This is between me and the girl," he replied.

Mr. Burton had made his way to the Bluffs in a small yellow dinghy that was now tied to a rock just behind the fishing boat we'd come in on. It had a small motor on it, which he must have turned very low when he made his way into the cavern. Either that, or he'd paddled his way in.

"I know you broke into my house and destroyed my bedroom," I said. "I found your library card.

You were looking for the other half of the map, weren't you?"

"You're smarter than I thought. I had the other half of that map for almost twenty years. I bought it from someone who found it in a bottle on the beach, but he said the other half was hidden in the library. I worked at that library every day trying to find that map, and you come in and find it without even trying!"

"Do you even like books?" I asked.

"Who cares about books?" Mr. Burton yelled. "I care about GOLD! I never wanted to work in that stupid library. I just wanted to be there every day so I could find the other half of the map before someone else did."

"And Cora found it," said Gerald, laughing at Mr. Burton.

"Well it doesn't matter much now, does it, because here we have the gold. This can't be all of it, but it's certainly enough for me to get far away from this ugly little town and start living the life I deserve!"

"Then take it," I said. "Take all of it and get out of here. We have no interest in the gold."

"We don't?" asked Gerald.

"It's not ours," I said. "We can't keep it."

Gerald looked terribly disappointed. "Oh," he said. "But maybe there is a reward."

"You can't get a reward for something you don't have," said Mr. Burton. "Since I am going to take the gold and skedaddle, you have nothing to claim. And just to make sure you don't try something foolish, like chase after me, I borrowed this from your boat."

He held up a large pile of rope that Gerald used to tie down cargo on his boat.

"Tie up the girl," he said, throwing the rope to Gerald.

Gerald looked at me and then at the rope in his hands. "I'm sorry, Cora," he said, "but he has a gun...."

"I understand."

I sat down on the ground with my back to a large rock and let Gerald tie me to it.

"When you're done with her," he said, "then I will tie you up."

Gerald tied the knots behind me tight enough that I would not be able to escape, but not so tight I was uncomfortable.

"That should do it," he said. "You're sure you're okay?"

"Yeah," I said.

Gerald then sat down beside me so Mr. Burton could proceed to tie him up. The entire time, Ethan stood watching everything, not sure what to make of this funny game. Calvin, surprisingly, had disappeared.

"You're not going to tie up a two-year-old, are you?" I asked Mr. Burton.

"No," he replied, "I'm going to take him with me!"

TWENTY-FIVE

"What?" I exclaimed. "You can't!"

"He's my insurance policy," he said. "I know you won't try anything stupid if I have him with me, and when I know I am out of danger, I will drop him off with a note to tell everyone where to find you two."

My worst nightmare. Mom had just started to trust me with Ethan alone and I was about to lose him to a gold-thieving librarian who hated books.

Mr. Burton pulled out a duffel bag and started to transfer as many of the gold bars as he could fit into it. After he had moved about ten of the bars, he dragged it down to where the boats were tied up, temporarily remaining out of site.

"Each one of those weighs close to thirty pounds," said Gerald. "He's not going to be able to carry very many of them in that little boat of his. It will sink."

"Sink?" I cried. "But he has Ethan with him."

This was shaping up to be a much more dangerous situation than I'd bargained for.

Mr. Burton returned with another bag and began to fill that one, too. When he'd put in another six or seven bars of gold, he zipped it up and started to drag it behind him.

"Come along now," said Mr. Burton in his librarian voice.

He took Ethan by the hand and started to lead him away from us. Ethan knew Mr. Burton well; he had often come with us to the library, so he didn't hesitate.

"Oh," said Mr. Burton, turning around. "If you don't mind, I'm going to take your boat. It's a bit faster."

Mr. Burton lifted the two duffel bags into the boat before climbing aboard with Ethan. We could only watch, helplessly tied to the rocks.

The engine of Gerald's boat roared to life and the boat slowly began to back out of the cavern. As Mr.

Burton pulled away, the light the spotlight had provided also dimmed. I could see Ethan on the front of the boat, waving goodbye to us, enjoying this game of hide-and-seek.

"Oh, Cora, what are we going to do?" asked Gerald. "We're both tied up, how can we get out of here?"

Neither of us could do anything, as we were both tied to the rock, but one of us was not tied to anything.

"Calvin!" I called. "Come here, buddy."

Calvin appeared from behind a small rock.

"Arr," he said, by way of greeting.

"Come here boy. Look," I said, trying to move my hands in a way that caught his attention. He cocked his head to one side and looked at me. I could tell he did not understand what I was trying to say.

"Look, look!" I said moving my hands faster. "Go get it!"

Calvin seemed to catch on at that moment and ran behind the rock to where my hands were tied. He started to chew on the rope like a new dog toy. He chewed through it enough to fray the rope to the point where I could slip out one hand and then the other.

"Good boy. I'm free," I said to Gerald. "I'll untie you."

"Reach into my pocket," he said. "There's a small pen-knife. You can use it to cut the rope."

I did as he suggested and found a small knife that made quick work of the rope. In just a few minutes, Gerald was free.

The three of us, including Calvin, ran down to where the small rubber dinghy was tied up.

"How fast do you think it can go?" I asked.

"Not very," he said. "Certainly not as fast as my boat."

We looked out at the water and could see Gerald's boat, now captained by Mr. Burton, quickly disappearing on the horizon.

"Let's not waste time," I said.

We climbed into the boat and proceeded to start the engine. After a few false starts, the small motor roared to life and we carefully navigated our way out of the cavern.

"I'm coming, Ethan," I said. "I'm coming to rescue you!"

TWENTY-SIX

Our small boat was indeed not much of a match for the larger fishing boat that Mr. Burton had stolen. We turned the speed up as far as it would go, but our small dinghy lagged farther and farther behind.

"Can this go any faster?" I asked.

"No, I'm afraid not," said Gerald.

"Arrrr," growled Calvin, obviously frustrated at our lack of speed.

We stayed on our course, trying our best to keep up with the larger boat, realizing the distance between us was growing with every wave we passed.

"It's no use," said Gerald. "We'll never catch them at this speed."

"Ahoy there!" yelled a voice.

We turned around and saw Mr. Morgan's large sailboat just behind us. On the stern of the boat waved Shelby and Tricia. Just behind them stood my very, *very*, angry mother.

"Look!" I yelled. "It's Mr. Morgan!"

The Morgans' boat pulled up beside us so we could climb up the small ladder that we used to climb aboard after diving off the back.

"I thought you could use a lift," said Mr. Morgan.

"How did you know we were here?" I asked, once the three of us were safely on board.

"Tricia and Shelby had the good sense to tell their parents what you were doing," bellowed my mother. "When they found out, they called me right away. What were you thinking?"

"I just wanted to find the treasure," I said. "And we did, it's back there."

Shelby's face lit up like a Christmas tree. "Are there diamonds and other jewels?"

"No, bars of gold. Tons and tons of gold bars. Some of it might still be on the boat. But Mr.

Burton took a lot of it with him. He stole Gerald's boat. We have to catch up to him."

"Where did you leave Ethan?" my mom asked. "Is he with Mrs. Trumble?"

I hesitated, but realized there was no way around it.

"He's with Mr. Burton," I replied. "He took Ethan with him."

I had never heard that register of my mother's voice before. It was strangely high-pitched and booming at the same time.

"WHHHAAATTTTTTTTTT?!" she howled.

"I'm sorry! He said it was his insurance policy."

I thought that since my mother was in the insurance business, this explanation might help to calm her down. It did not.

"What on earth were you thinking?!"

She ran to the steering wheel of the boat, pushing Mr. Morgan aside and pulling the throttle to full. The boat surged forward, knocking Tricia and me to the floor.

"Here," said Mr. Morgan. "Let me. I think I can handle it."

"Just get them!"

The boat raced forward, quickly gaining on the small fishing boat ahead of us.

"Cora," my Mother said. "What you did was very dangerous and extremely careless! What if something happens to Ethan?"

"You're right," I apologized. "You're right. I shouldn't have brought him with me."

"You shouldn't have come at all! This is far too dangerous for anyone! You should have told the police and let them investigate it!"

"Cora," said Shelby. "Tell me about the gold. Did you take any with you?"

"No," I replied. "We didn't have time."

"There is *always* time for gold!"

"How did you find this place?" asked Tricia.

"There were two parts to the map. When I saw the whole map, I knew the treasure had to be somewhere in a place called the Three Wise Men. That's where we were," I said.

I turned to my mother, feeling I owed her as much explanation as possible. "It was Mr. Burton who broke into our house. He was looking for the other part of the map."

"Jake," said my mom to Mr. Morgan. "Can you radio the police? Ask them to call Officer Orzabal and tell him what's going on?"

"Already on it," he said, reaching for the radio.

As Mr. Morgan radioed the police, the fishing

boat grew larger, the distance between us decreasing.

"Not far now," I said. "We'll catch up with him soon."

TWENTY-SEVEN

"Your boat has some serious power," said Mr. Morgan to Gerald.

"I spent a fortune upgrading the engine last year," he said. "Money well spent, apparently."

As the distance between the two boats grew smaller, we could see Mr. Burton's face grow more and more alarmed. He was not counting on a large sailboat catching up with him and his stolen gold bars.

"Ethan!" my Mom yelled from the side of the ship. "It's Mommy!"

Ethan waved at our mother, happy to see she

was participating in our fun little adventure.

"What is he doing?" asked Tricia.

Mr. Burton had started to turn the boat back towards us, and was coming up to the side of the boat. He was aiming the fishing boat right at us!

"Is he crazy?" asked Mr. Morgan as we watched Mr. Burton slam the fishing boat into the side of Mr. Morgan's ship.

"You're going to kill us all!" yelled Mr. Morgan. "Frank! Do you hear me? Stop slamming the boats or we'll all drown!"

"The police are coming! You won't get away with this!" my mother yelled. "You can't kidnap a child and expect to get away with it!"

"I don't care about the kid," he shouted. "He's unharmed! Let me go and I'll give him back in return."

"Pull up around the back!" yelled Mr. Morgan.

Mr. Burton did as Mr. Morgan said, and pulled the boat up to the back of the Morgans' boat. We were close enough for my mother to jump over to Gerald's boat and grab Ethan. She hugged him tightly, much to the impatience of Mr. Burton.

"Take him and go!" he yelled.

My mother stood up with Ethan in her arms and climbed back onto the Morgans' boat. No sooner had she stepped aboard than Mr. Burton roared away again, trying to distance himself from us as quickly as possible.

"Fun!" cried Ethan, clearly enjoying himself.

Calvin, happy to see Ethan again, ran over to him and started licking his face, causing Ethan to fall to the floor of the boat in a fit of laughter.

"He's getting away!" called Tricia.

"Not for long, look," I said, pointing to a speedboat quickly approaching from another direction. "Police Marine Unit" was written on the side. "The police are here!"

We could see Officer Orzabal yelling instructions to the captain of the boat, making sure he pursued the right craft.

The police boat grew closer to the fishing boat, which was clearly not matched for speed.

"Hold it there, Burton!" called Officer Orzabal from the loudspeaker of the police boat. "Turn yourself in before anyone gets hurt."

"Never!" yelled the librarian. I could see him picking up one of the bags of gold from the boat and, clutching it tightly to his chest, he jumped overboard into the water.

His attempt to swim was pointless; the gold weighed far too much and was starting to pull him under. He flailed around in the water, his head bobbing above and below the waves.

"Frank!" called Officer Orzabal. "You're going to drown! Drop the gold!"

"Never!" Mr. Burton yelled.

"You'll drown!" yelled Gerald. "For Pete's sake, drop the bag!"

Mr. Burton must have realized it was either going to be his life or the gold, so he dropped the bag and started to tread water, trying to keep himself afloat.

"It's gone," he cried.

The police boat pulled up beside him and Officer Orzabal, with the assistance of another officer, was able to pull him safely onboard.

"Frank Burton," the officer said. "You're under arrest."

TWENTY-EIGHT

Back at the docks, Mr. Burton had been handcuffed and pushed up against the back of the police car, its lights flashing. The second officer who had accompanied Officer Orzabal wrote down some information on a clipboard as Mr. Burton rolled his eyes in disbelief.

We had all made it back to the dock safely. Gerald's fishing boat was docked in his slip, but as it still had one of the two bags of gold on it, it was off-limits. Yellow police tape surrounded it to keep anyone from boarding.

"How long will I be without my boat?" he asked

Officer Orzabal.

"Not too long, Gerald. We'll try to keep the investigation short. Maybe a week, two at most."

"Two weeks?" he cried. "What am I going to do for two weeks?

"Take a vacation. Enjoy it!"

Gerald did not look happy. "Take a vacation? I have *never* taken a vacation. Hey, wait a minute. That's not a bad idea. Hey everyone, I'm taking a vacation!"

We laughed at his excitement, happy that he was able to find a silver lining in the situation.

"I don't think the damage is too bad," said Mr. Morgan, inspecting the part of his boat Mr. Burton had rammed with the fishing boat.

"Insurance should cover it," my Mom said with a smile.

"What is going to happen to the rest of the gold?" asked Shelby, anxious to get back on the boat to collect the rest of the bars.

"The police will send over some investigators, I suppose. They'll see how much is left and work with the officials to determine who owns the gold."

"But Cora found it," said Tricia. "It's hers!"

"I don't think that's how it works, unfortunately," my mom said. "It belongs to the company that was shipping it, if they're still around. Fortunately, gold is worth far more today than it was then, so they'll be happy to know it has been recovered."

"You know who else is going to be happy?" I asked. "Maggie."

***

"Come in, come in," said Maggie, ushering me into her living room.

The day after the most exciting Sunday I'd ever had, I called Maggie to ask if I could stop by her place to see her. The news of what happened the previous day was all over town. The local paper dedicated four full pages to the story, which was one too many in my opinion. They'd even reprinted the treasure map in full color.

"Thank you," I said, taking a seat on her sofa.

"I just can't believe everything I've been hearing," she said. "I can't believe the boat has been discovered after all these years."

"It must be nice to know what happened, even though it didn't turn out very well," I said.

"Oh, you're wrong, it did turn out well. It's a terrible tragedy that I lost Lyle, but at least I know he did not pirate that ship and take off with stolen gold. I know he died trying to save his fellow sailors. He's a hero."

"I found this in the cavern," I said. "It's for you."

I produced the handwritten note from Lyle that I'd found in the bottle.

"I need my specs," she said, reaching for her eyeglasses that were dangling from a chain around her neck. "Let's see here...."

She began to read the letter and a small tear appeared on the side of her eye and rolled down her cheek.

"Oh, Lyle," she said, holding the note to her chest. "He cared enough to write to me, even at the end."

"I have something else for you," I said, producing a letter from my bag.

"Two letters? My goodness, I never get this much mail!"

She took the letter from my hands and inspected the envelope. "What is this?"

"It's from the insurance company. Now that they know what happened to the gold, and to Lyle, they're going to pay out the life insurance and you can keep your house."

"But how..." she stammered.

"My mother works for the insurance company," I explained. "She experit... expeti..."

"*Expedited*?" said Maggie.

"Yes. Made it go faster."

My mother had worked all day Monday to have the claim settled, and the letter explained to Maggie that her claim would be paid out within seven days.

"Oh, Cora, that's marvelous. I can't thank you enough for all your help."

"You're welcome," I said, "but I have a request to make. I need your help with something."

TWENTY-NINE

A week later, the day of our presentations at school arrived. I'd decided to have some guest speakers: Gerald Pape, Maggie Gordon, Mr. Morgan, Officer Orzabal, and my mother accompanied me to school to talk about what had happened on the day of our adventure. Even Calvin came along.

Most of the class already knew what happened that day, but they were happy to hear the story first-hand.

"And then we yelled at him to drop the gold," said Officer Orzabal.

"Did he?" asked Alex Bass.

"Yes, absolutely. He would have drowned otherwise."

"So where is the gold now?" asked Jimmy Carson.

"At the bottom of the river," I answered.

The glass gasped at this statement, as each of them considered how to get to the bottom of the river to recover the gold.

"Don't even think about it," said Gerald. "You'll never be able to find it. And even if you did, it would be too heavy to carry up to the surface."

"What about the other gold? Where is that?" asked someone in the class.

Officer Orzabal stood up. "All of the gold that was recovered at the site of the crash has been moved to a vault until the investigation concludes. We are speaking with representatives from the company that was shipping the gold and making sure that this belongs to them. It will probably be returned to them in the end."

"Does Cora get any of it?" asked Jimmy.

"No," I answered. "Sorry, Jimmy."

"Don't apologize to me," he said. "You're the one who doesn't have any gold."

I explained to the class that Mr. Burton had

made a full confession and was being totally cooperative. He was expected to serve time in jail, but since the trial was still another few weeks away, no one knew how much time he would serve.

At the end of my presentation, the class clapped loudly and even gave me a standing ovation! I was a little embarrassed, but only for a minute.

"Thank you, Cora," said Mr. Levine. "We'll take a few minutes' break, if you want to ask our guests more questions."

Many of the students got out of their seats and ran up to my guests to ask more questions. They wanted to know more details, even though my presentation covered most of what happened.

"You realize," said Shelby to me, "that I have to present now. I have to go up there and talk about Vegetables."

"I'm sure it will go very well," I said, only half-believing it.

"Yeah, right," she said, turning away from me. As she was about to walk away, she turned around and said, "That was really good Cora, and I'm glad you're safe."

"Thanks," I said, smiling.

"Next time maybe I'll come with you. But you can bet I'll take some of the gold for myself."

She winked and walked away.

"I'm still mad at you," said my Mother as she walked over to me. "What you did was very dangerous, not only for you, but for Ethan, Calvin and poor Gerald. You all could have been killed!"

"I know," I said. Even though I had apologized ninety-nine times since, I decided to make it an even one hundred. "I'm sorry."

"I have thought about your punishment, and I've decided to take away your Internet privileges. You will still be allowed to use the computer for school research, but no video chatting with Shelby or Tricia."

Even thought it was a punishment, I thought it was fair, and was fairly certain I would be able to manage without video chat for a while.

"How long?"

"A month. But we'll see. Maybe I'll give you time off for good behavior."

"Okay," I replied, hugging my mother around her waist.

I suddenly remembered something. "What happened this morning with your case?" I asked.

My mother had finished her investigation on the accident claim insurance with the busload of people. She'd filed her report and they'd made the final decision that very morning.

"We denied everything," she announced. "Not a cent will go to any of the people on the bus. I visited the other people who were on the claim and found they were also lying. They weren't even hurt, and were walking around and functioning just like nothing happened."

"Did you find out who was behind it?" I asked.

"You'll never guess," she said. "It was the bus driver! I started to investigate him on a hunch, and it turned out that he'd done the same thing in two different cities before he lived here. Those claims were successful, but the insurance company is going to reopen the investigations on those. He was the mastermind behind the whole thing, along with the person driving the car they hit. The two of them paid all of the people on the bus to lie, and were going to split the money. It was a big scam!"

"I'm so happy you figured it out!" I said. "Your first case is solved!"

I high-fived my mom must as Mr. Levine walked over.

"Cora," he said. "Do you have a moment?"

"Sure."

"Now, you didn't exactly follow instructions for your assignment."

I was afraid of this. Even though my subject was "Local shipping trade", I had veered off course a little bit, but I thought since my story was so exciting and unusual, the teacher would overlook it.

"I know, but I was hoping you would take everything into consideration."

He smiled and nodded. "Of course. But next time, try to follow directions. It might be a little less dangerous."

"I'll try," I said, not sure I would be able to follow through with that promise.

Mr. Levine turned to walk away but stopped and looked back, "Oh," he said. "A. Plus."

This was not the first A+ I'd received, but somehow this one felt like I'd earned it. More special this time. Good as gold.

ABOUT THE AUTHOR

Tommy Davey spent his youth writing mystery stories and plays, and watching reruns of Three's Company until every line of dialogue was permanently burned into his memory. When not writing, he enjoys traveling to favorite destinations including New York City and Paris, which he plans to feature in future stories. He lives in Toronto, where he was born and raised, with a Norfolk Terrier named Calvin.

Made in the USA
Charleston, SC
14 December 2012